MONSTER ZOMBIES

Are

Coming for Johnny

~~~~~~~~~~

A.M. SHAH

99 Pages or Less Publishing, LLC

© 2016 by Aarambh Shah All rights reserved.
First Edition, 2016

Published by 99 Pages or Less Publishing, LLC
Miami, FL
For inquiries email: info@99pagesorless.com

Printed in the United States of America
10 9 8 7 6 5 4 3 2 1

Cover Illustration by: Pedro Demetriou
Typesetting by: Mandi Cofer

Library of Congress Cataloging-in-Publication Data is available for this title.

Library of Congress Control Number: 2016908055

ISBN: 978-1-943684-19-9 (hc); ISBN: 978-1-943684-18-2 (sc);
ISBN: 978-1-943684-20-5 (e)

To Ashton
and Ashley.

~~~~~~~~

The monsters
are coming!

CONTENTS

~~~~~~~~~~

CHAPTER
1

~~~~~~~~~~

*S*cratch, scratch, scratch . . .

Johnny woke up dripping with sweat. "Momma!" he cried out and waited for Momma to come to the room. Louder he shouted and louder he cried. Five minutes passed, and no one came. The light bulbs on the fan above him flickered on. On his left, the closet doorknob turned to the right exactly one time.

BAAAM!

Johnny's books hit the floor beside his nightstand. Johnny, as scared as he could be, stopped crying. He sat up in bed, and with his back to the headboard, he heard the sound again.

Scratch, scratch, scratch . . .

"**AHHHH**," Johnny screamed as a green shadow glowed through the black crack of the closet door. All of a sudden, Johnny felt dizzy. His eyes drooped. Within seconds his chin hit the center of his chest. He passed out.

CHAPTER

2

~~~~~~~~

Good morning, honey," Johnny's mom said with a cheerful smile as she walked into his room. "You're not going to believe this, but I got my second interview at . . ." As she started to speak, she noticed that Johnny was dripping wet. "Oh, my! What happened?" she asked.

Johnny awoke from his sleep and shouted, "Momma! Momma!" He crawled into her arms.

"What happened, baby?"

"There was a green monster in the closet, and he was coming for me."

"Oh, Johnny, which closet? This one?"

Johnny opened his eyes fully and yelled, "No, Mom! Don't go in there!"

As Janie opened the closet, a green bathrobe hanging from the top shelf hit the floor. **PLUNK**

"You see, baby? Now, come on. Get changed. We are late for school," his mom said.

Johnny was relieved. It was just a nightmare. "Okay, Momma."

So, little Johnny got dressed as usual. First, he took off his pajamas and underwear. Then, he reached for his fresh, new clothes: underwear, pants, and red, button-up, uniform shirt. He quickly put on his socks and shoes and headed for the door. As he was about to shut the door and leave, he heard the eerie sound again:

Scratch, scratch, scratch.

Johnny quickly ran through the hallway, nearly stepping on Jafree's tail, the fluffy orange cat, lying curled up by the baseboards.

Wooosh.

Johnny slid between his momma's legs and held on tight. "Momma I heard a noise."

"Johnny, don't be scared. It's just the wind.

Look outside, today is a windy day." Indeed, it was. As Johnny looked outside his living room window, he saw the trees rustle and the littered paper from the street drift off, side by side, in front of a yellow school bus.

"Oh, look, Johnny, perfect timing. The bus is here."

CHAPTER

3

~~~~~~~~~

The bus door creaked open, and a smelly gust of sneakers and sweat hit Johnny in the face. "Ewww," Johnny said while pinching his nose.

"Well, are you coming in or are you just going to stand there?" said Ms. Eisenstein, the sixty-four-year-old bus driver.

Johnny looked at the tiny whiskers poking out of her wrinkly skin and said, "Yes, Ms. Eisenstein."

"Well, hurry on up. We're late, you hear?" she barked.

Johnny hopped on the bus and walked to the back. "Woah" he said to himself while holding onto the ripped cushion seat to catch his balance as the bus started to move.

"Why is no one on the bus?" Johnny thought. "Oh, I see Alex sweet," he said as he walked more confidently towards the back.

"What's up Alex? What did your mom give you for lunch today?" No response from Alex. "Hellooo?" No response again.

Alex stared at the seat in front of him. His neon green backpack was tightly wrapped around his scrawny shoulder blades. His large green eyes were open and looked straight through his extra thick glasses directly into the yellow-gray hole in the seat cushion in front of him.

Johnny touched Alex's right arm. "Hey, man."

Nothing.

Johnny tapped Alex's arm and finally pinched it. No response. Johnny sat across the aisle from him. Slowly, with one hand grabbing the green seat cushion in front of him and his other hand holding onto his backpack strap, he stared at Alex as the bumpy ride took them to school.

CHAPTER

4

~~~~~~~~~~

The bus arrived at Sandy Furlow Middle School. "Ok boys, time to get out," Ms. Eisenstein said with a cracked and creepy voice. She yanked on a lever and a muffled, harangued, trumpeting erupted as the doors opened.

"What the!" Alex said grabbing both ears.

"Dude, where were you?"

"Huh?" Alex responded.

"Out. Now!" Ms. Eisenstein barked again while mumbling something else.

Both Johnny and Alex looked at each other, stood up, tightened their backpack straps and walked towards the front of the bus. "Bye, Ms. Eisenstein," Johnny replied looking out the door at the frosty day.

"Yeah, yeah, hurry up, you two." She huffed as they stepped down the bus steps to the cracked concrete that led them to the large front doors of Sandy Furlow.

As they arrived at the large, wooden, eight-foot-tall doors, Johnny looked back. Ms. Eisenstein and the yellow bus were completely gone. "Wow! That was fast." He reached for the front doorknob. The doors to the school were not only shut, but they were also locked. Neither Johnny nor Alex could understand why.

"Is today a holiday?" Alex asked.

"No," Johnny replied.

"Are you sure? Maybe they announced a new holiday, and we didn't pay attention. Teachers always tell me I don't pay attention enough."

"There is no holiday, Alex. This is just . . ."

A moving shadow caught the corner of Johnny's eye. He looked toward the mushroom style bushes near the right side of the doors. The bushes lined the perimeter of the school. On his tippy-toes, he peeked over them and noticed a lone figure standing in the middle of the deserted playground. The figure's back was turned to the boys. "Weird."

Alex walked towards Johnny to see what was up. "Who's that?"

"I don't know," Johnny answered, barely hearing the question.

"From behind it looks kind of like Billy Tilden," Johnny added.

"That's not Billy Tilden."

Johnny squeezed through two green mushroom bushes and walked toward the motionless figure. As he got closer, he noticed a red varsity jacket, blue jeans and muddy white sneakers. Alex hesitated.

"Maybe we should just leave him alone." Alex swallowed, nervous for some unknown reason. "He looks like he's concentrating on something."

Johnny didn't listen to Alex. He kept

walking until he was only a few feet from whomever it was. Even with Johnny so close, the mysterious person remained as still as a statue.

"Hey," Johnny barked at the figure. Still nothing. Johnny peeked back at Alex, who was squinting through the mushroom bushes watching with both hands cupping his eyes. Johnny addressed the stranger's back again. He was staring into space past the playground.

"Do you know where everyone is?"

"Ask him if today's a new holiday we don't know about," Alex yelled.

"It's *not* a holiday, Alex!" Johnny snapped back.

When Johnny turned his head back toward the figure, it was standing a nose distance apart from him. Johnny's eyes widened and he turned white as he tilted his head back. Alex froze with fear.

CHAPTER

5

At first, Johnny couldn't make sense of what he was seeing, although, it made him shiver. The face looked human . . . once. But all the color in its skin was gone, leaving it a cold gray. The eyes had no life in them, yet they still managed to see. The dark black circles around the eye sockets looked like the depths of outer space. Green slime oozed out the sides as two white eyeballs splashed slowly, side-to-side, in the sockets. Johnny could feel their glare.

Alex wanted to yell at Johnny to run. But he was so struck with fear that nothing would come out of his mouth. The only sound in the air was the breeze blowing. Then the creature licked its rotten, bottom, bony lip, and Johnny once again heard the eerie sound:

Scratch, scratch, scratch.

Next, the monstrous figure moved. It took one, long, slow step toward Johnny as he took one quick step backwards. As it planted its foot in the dirt, you could hear its bones shift. Before it could take another step, Johnny and Alex were off, running and screaming. They were looking for somewhere to hide and someone to help them.

They ran around the other side of the school building without daring to look back. Finally, after making their way to the back of the school building, they stopped to take a breath. Neither of them could make sense of what they saw.

"What . . ." Johnny wheezed and bent over with both hands on his knees.

"Was that?" Alex finished.

"It's a zombie," said a voice.

"You think so?" Alex asked Johnny looking down.

"Do I think what? I didn't say it was a zombie, you did."

"That wasn't me."

The boys looked around.

"Well, if it wasn't you," Johnny said.

"And if it wasn't you," Alex said.

"Then it must have been me!" said a strange voice in a high-pitched sound. A figure stepped out from behind the mushroom bushes.

"AHHHH," the boys screamed.

"Please don't eat me!" Alex cried ducking down with one arm covering his eyes.

With one knee bent to the ground, Johnny froze in shock, staring at a whistle swinging side to side in front of a white sport shirt.

The boys looked up and saw it was Coach McGinty from the basketball team. Both Johnny and Alex were laughed out of tryouts, so this was the first time Coach ever spoke to them directly.

"Are you boys alright?" Coach McGinty asked hastily.

Before the boys answered, they looked closer at Coach and noticed dirt and grass stains all over his white, tucked-in, collar shirt. His white socks, full of green stains, almost touched his swollen kneecaps. He was sweaty too.

"Are you *okay?*" Coach McGinty asked again, urgently.

"No . . . I mean, yes," Johnny replied while struggling to stand up.

"I've had a bad cough lately," Alex added.

"I meant have you boys been bitten by any of these…whatever they are?"

"Zombies?" Johnny asked.

Coach bent forward from the waist and grabbed Johnny by the collar with his two hands. "There are no such things as zombies!" Coach let go, wiped his sweaty brow and patted Johnny on the shoulder while looking behind him. Johnny could see that Coach McGinty was scared. In his mind, he was questioning everything he once thought was real.

"Where did everybody go?" Johnny asked the Coach.

"They're gone," Coach responded, his eyes darting around, looking out for danger.

"Gone?" Alex questioned. "Oh, noooo . . ."

Johnny started to fire questions at Coach McGinty. "You mean . . ."

"They escaped."

"Where?"

"How?"

"Who?"

Scratch, scratch, scratch.

Just as Coach McGinty was about to answer, a hand reached out of the mushroom bushes behind him and grabbed his shoulder.

The boys screamed and jumped back. Then, another hand took hold of Coach's forearm as his whistle wrapped around his tire belly. "**Ahhhhhh!**" Coach yelled trying to get out of the grip while hands grabbed both kneecaps and yanked him to the ground headfirst.

PLANK!

"Ouch! Please . . . I beg you, don't . . . Run, boys, run!!!" he eked out as he got pulled into the bushes. All that remained were Coach's hand prints from wrestling in the dirt and a slimy green blob that mirrored Coach's broken-off whistle.

CHAPTER

6

~~~~~~~~~

Run, Alex! Run as fast as you can!" Johnny screamed as his heart was pounding and his legs were shuffling.

"No, not that way, Johnny. Come this way!" Alex yelled pointing at the back door to the gym.

As Johnny caught up, they saw the back entrance slightly open. "Go in!" Johnny yelled, out of breath, pressing his knees again and almost fell over.

"Uhhh, no way! You go," Alex replied.

"Fine. Come on," Johnny snapped at Alex. "Into the gym. We have to regroup."

The boys entered the school's large two-story gymnasium. There were no sounds to be heard from anywhere on the second floor. They peeked down from the balcony and glanced at the basketball rims on either side of the wooden floors. The gym looked to be deserted. "This way . . . Let's go down there. I think I see someone," Johnny whispered and off they went on their tippy-toes to the side door.

They made their way down the staircase to the front door of the gym on the ground floor. Johnny peeked through the rectangular window panel in the wooden door and took in a close-up view of the stadium-style, dark, wooden bleachers. His nose left a smear on the window panel. Alex stood quietly behind him, unsure of what to do. Johnny then pressed his thumb down on the silver door handle and creaked the door open.

"Is the coast clear?" Alex mumbled, hoping the answer was "yes."

"I think so."

"I don't hear anything,"

"That's what I'm worried about."

"You think Coach McGinty is alright?" Alex asked with a cracked voice.

Johnny looked at Alex. Alex's eyes filled with worry. Johnny didn't have the heart to tell him what he thought the truth was.

"He's a big, strong guy," Johnny finally said. "I'm sure he can take care of himself."

Johnny could see that Alex wasn't convinced. Johnny gave Alex a reassuring pat on the shoulder and opened the gym door about halfway. He listened for a second, heard nothing, and then entered first. Alex followed behind him.

Scratch, scratch, scratch

As they walked towards the basketball net on the east side, they came to a dead stop.

Before their eyes, sitting in the front seats on the sidelines at about half court, were dozens of these monsters, these zombies. They were staring off into space as if they were in a military, waiting to take orders.

Johnny stopped breathing. His heart sank to the floor. He could hear Alex's teeth chatter in the pure silence. Johnny, with his finger to his lips, nodded to Alex, urging him to back out of the auditorium.

"Where did they come from?" Johnny whispered.

"Uh, don't know, man," Alex said as he wiped fog from his glasses.

"Shhhhhh, Alex! Let's get out of here."

"Oh, boy, this is real. We're dead. I don't want to . . ." Petrified, Alex started hissing through his teeth.

Before Alex could finish his sentence he knocked into a set of metal, folding chairs leaned up against the black drapes. It barely registered a sound, but one of the zombie monsters sitting in the center of the court turned his head towards the west court, then did a fast 90-degree turn, locking eyes with Alex.

CHAPTER

7

~~~~~~~~~~

A second later, all of the folding chairs against the wall fell, crashing to the floor one after the other. The impact caught the attention of every zombie in the auditorium. Hundreds more originated from a green colored mist that seemed to appear out of nowhere but emerged from the fox logo in the center of the court. Alex and Johnny then did what they were quickly becoming experts at—they ran.

As the clumsy creatures lurched forward, they started tripping over the fallen chairs. That gave Johnny and Alex enough time to storm out of the school building, off the school grounds, and down the street.

They were yelling for help without any response. Alex peeked back, only to see the horde of zombies following them.

"Look," Johnny yelled. He saw Ms.

Eisenstein's bus parked ahead by the Sandy Furlow Quickie Mart.

Ms. Eisenstein was eating a sandwich, reading the newspaper and listening to her favorite jam. The music prevented her from hearing Alex and Johnny screaming her name at the top of their lungs. It was only when they crashed against the bus's front door that she looked up. With an angry, confused expression she opened the door. As the harsh trumpet sound erupted she yelled, "What are you kids . . ."

But before she could finish, Alex and Johnny were already in her face holding on to their backpack straps.

"Drive!" Johnny yelled and pointed to the street.

"Who do you think you are talking to like that, young man?" said Ms. Eisenstein, wiping away the spilled peanut butter stain from her exposed thighs.

Then came a hard thump against the back of the bus.

Scratch, scratch, scratch.

CHAPTER
8

What in the world is that?" Ms. Eisenstein asked, startled.

Alex shook.

Johnny answered. "It's them."

Ms. Eisenstein glanced in her side-view mirror that read: "Objects seem closer than they appear." She didn't know what she saw, but it scared her like never before. She closed the door just in time as several zombies pressed against it, frothing at their mouths.

They were gray with green slime hanging from their skin, which had large crater-sized holes. Their jaws slanted to the left or right, and their teeth were exposed as if something rotten had eaten at their lips and gums. Their eyes popped out of their sockets, and they looked to be eight feet tall with their heads almost scraping against the top of the bus.

All three of them screamed. Ms. Eisenstein

turned on the engine and hit the gas as hard as she could.

As the last of the zombies shrunk in the rearview mirror, the boys breathed a small sigh of relief. However, they noticed Ms. Eisenstein's thoughts were scrambled.

"Who? What?" she asked. "How?"

"They were zombies, Ms. Eisenstein," Johnny said holding onto the seat cushion behind her.

"Zombies!" Alex added.

"You didn't notice anything this morning?" Johnny asked her.

"This morning?" she asked.

"You didn't see where everyone went?"

"I . . . zombies . . ." Ms. Eisenstein was too shaken to talk.

"We should drive into town," Johnny suggested. "Go to the police station. They probably already know what's happening."

"What about our parents?" Alex asked.

Johnny hadn't even thought about that. Mom was home, last he knew. Dad was at work, so he thought. He had to get in touch with at least one of them, somehow, at some point.

"I'm sure they'll let us use the phone at the station," Johnny told Alex.

"AAAAAAAAAAH!"

The screeching breaks accompanied Ms. Eisenstein's scream. The boys dived forward against the black panel with Ms. Eisenstein's chubby calves in sight. The bus stopped.

The boys backs smarted from the impact but were in okay shape. They got their bearings, stood up, and looked out through the front windshield.

CHAPTER

9

~~~~~~~~

The view down Cedar Avenue was something out of a nightmare. The street, which led straight to the plaza in the center of town, was overrun with slow-walking zombie monsters. They were staggering this way and that way. They seemed to have no particular direction. There was a strange, evil purpose driving their movements. None, thankfully, were aware of the spectators on the bus.

"This must be a bad dream," Ms. Eisenstein said out loud to herself. "I must be sleeping. That's it. I'm asleep right now."

"I wish that were true," Johnny told her. "But you're not. None of us are."

"Fast asleep, in my safe little beddy-by," the shell-shocked bus driver continued. She was talking madly as if no one else was there.

Johnny and Alex turned to each other.

"I think she's lost it," Alex said.

"Wouldn't you?" Johnny responded.

There was a pause.

"I'm scared," Alex said.

"I know," Johnny replied. "So am I."

Johnny looked out again. The situation remained the same.

Then Alex spoke with excitement in his voice. "Look. Up there." He pointed. "On the roof!"

They saw someone on the roof of the Central Bank building, in a shirt and tie with rolled up sleeves. He was waving frantically, trying to get the bus's attention.

"I don't think he's a zombie," Alex yelled.

"He's not."

The man pointed out over the little league field toward the forest on the fringes of town. All three pairs of eyes tried to see what the man was gesturing to.

Then Johnny saw smoke. Smoke from a

controlled fire of some sort. "He's pointing over there. The fire. That must be where everyone in town ran away to."

"Why do you say that?" Alex asked.

"Because my dad always told me, if there's ever major flooding in the town, head to the high ground in the woods."

"But this isn't a flood," Alex said.

"Not of water," Johnny responded, followed by a knowing pause.

"So, then, why the fire?" Alex continued.

"Only guess that makes sense," Johnny replied, "Maybe zombies don't like fire?"

"Great. To the fire then, that's settled." Ms. Eisenstein yelled. With both fists, she turned the large steering wheel completely around with all her might as the bus turned off Cedar Avenue onto Brook Street.

CHAPTER
10
~~~~~~~~

Wait!" Johnny yelled waving his hands in front of Ms. Eisenstein. "We have to save him first." She hit the brakes immediately.

"Save him?" she asked. "How? He's on the roof, and all those horrible creatures are close to him."

"If it was you up there, would you want us to leave you?" Johnny replied.

This thought made Ms. Eisenstein put the gear back in drive and drift slowly toward the bank. "I guess not," she replied before stopped completely in front of the Central Bank building.

The zombie monsters now looked even larger and scarier as they were zigzagging across the brick paved street by the large waterfall fountain in the center of the plaza about fifteen yards away from the bank.

Johnny looked up at the man stranded on the roof. He was still frantic, this time holding up one finger and gesturing with his hands to stay put. He then turned around and disappeared from view.

"Just wait," Johnny said. "He's trying to sneak down to us now."

Ms. Eisenstein sighed impatiently. She put the bus in park. Her right leg started shaking as she folded her arms. The boys kept one eye on the entrance to the bank building and another on the scattering of zombies at the fountain in front of them. The monsters were still oblivious to their presence.

Johnny took this time to wonder. "Where did they all come from?"

"I don't know," Alex said. "But they should go back."

"They must have been regular people once.

That's why this place looks like a ghost town. Johnny replied. That's the only explanation."

"Nothing makes sense anymore." Alex shook his head slowly.

"Maybe a zombie, I don't know," Johnny started, "can turn another person *into* a zombie? Put them in some kind of trance."

"Trance?" Alex asked.

"Like where your mind is not yours anymore. Actually, earlier on the bus when I got on . . . you looked like you were in some sort of trance."

"Me?"

"Yeah."

Alex reflected. "You know, I don't remember the bus ride before you got on."

"Did you, by chance," Johnny said, "Hear scratching at any point? This morning? Like a 'scratch, scratch, scratch?' Against a window or a wall?"

Ms. Eisenstein glanced in the rear view mirror curiously. Alex thought some more.

Suddenly, a large nose hit the back right side of the passenger bus window.

BAAM!

The boys ran towards the back of the bus through the narrow walkway between the seat cushions and looked out the window. It was the man on the roof. His tie was loose, and his white-collar shirt was untucked at one side. His hair was frazzled, losing the comb-over it once had. Sweat formed on his forehead, soaked through his collar and left a puddle stain under each armpit.

He examined his immediate surroundings before fully emerging from behind the door. He looked left, then right, and then left again. Finally, he ran lightning fast toward the front of the bus with the boys following his pace from the inside. As he ran to the front, Ms.

Eisenstein squeezed the handle to open the door in anticipation.

"Hurry, hurry," Johnny said.

"I think he's going to make it," said Alex.

And he almost did.

Almost.

But before he could get to the door . . .

Scratch, scratch, scratch.

The big-nosed man was tackled by something unseen.

Ms. Eisenstein screamed at the top of her lungs while letting go of the door handle and speeding off. The boys ran to the back of the bus to see what happened to him, as the bus turned onto Pike Street.

All they could see were his legs dangling followed by a complete pause. His entire body was covered with creatures hovering over him stomping on his back. Seconds later his legs were out of sight, and the only thing that remained outside the pile of gray, green, bony zombie creatures were his two brown oxford shoes lying on the concrete.

CHAPTER
11

Johnny and Alex walked to the front of the bus and sat next to each other behind Ms. Eisenstein. Johnny looked out the window and noticed that there wasn't another car driving on the road. Because of this, Ms. Eisenstein only paused at red lights and blew right by stop signs.

"Put your seatbelts on," she said at one point. The boys obeyed, as the ride got bumpy. They were already near the outer part of town, about to enter the roadway leading into the woods.

Soon the black smoke rising above the forest trees was closer. They could smell the burning wood. Johnny turned his head and saw Alex's head tilted down against the bus window. He put his arm around his sad, frightened friend. "We're going to get out of this. We're going to find our family and friends. We're going to be alright."

Alex looked up at Johnny, appreciating the words but not ready to believe them. But he knew he had to try to believe them anyways.

CHAPTER
12
~~~~~~~~

It was green," Johnny continued. He was telling Alex about what he saw in his closet that morning. "I thought it was a dream. I *hoped* it was a dream."

"But it wasn't?" Alex asked.

"No. It wasn't."

Ms. Eisenstein continued navigating the bus through the thin, woodland road while frequently glancing in the rearview mirror. The sides of the oversized vehicle were getting stained and scratched by forest overhang. The ride was mostly quiet the rest of the way. Ms. Eisenstein tried driving over an elevated tree root as opposed to around it. Fear had affected her judgment.

Soon the tire dislodged, and the bus tipped, throwing the boys this way and that way, their seat belts holding strong. Ms. Eisenstein lost control and careened directly into a tree.

"Oh, no! Ms. Eisenbagel flattened our tires," Alex smirked.

"I heard that!" she barked, looking at them in the rearview mirror.

After a moment, in which they collected themselves, the battered trio looked at each other to make sure they weren't hurt. There was no major damage, thankfully. The boys unbuckled their seat belts and stood up.

"Stay on the bus!" Ms. Eisenstein rasped, wiping sweat from her chubby brow. "Just *remain in the* bus for now!"

"We can't stay here," Johnny said. "We have to get to the fire. We can walk from here."

"We are not walking out there, young man!"

"So we're just going to stay on the bus forever?"

"I don't know which is worse," Alex said.

A moment of silence passed.

"I think you should open this door," Johnny said.

"Ha! You're dreaming," Ms. Eisenstein responded.

"Alex, you see anything out there?"

Alex was scouting the area from the back of the bus. He tried catching movement in the woods. The zombie shadows moved slowly making the leaves shake every couple of seconds. Then instinct drove them to pounce.

"I don't know," Alex finally answered.

"Well, do you see a zombie-monster?"

"No."

"So, then, the coast is clear?"

Alex paused. "Maybe."

Suddenly, a sound erupted from underneath their feet.

Scratch, scratch, scratch.

Johnny stared at the green ooze foaming

up into the middle of the bus. His eyes widened. Again . . .

Scratch, scratch, scratch.

All three of them were stunned into silence.

Scratch, scratch, scratch . . . Scratch, scratch, scratch.

All of a sudden a huge, greenish fist broke through the middle of the bus floor. They all screamed. Johnny glanced back at Ms. Eisenstein, but she was gone. Only Johnny, Alex, and the green fist was left.

Johnny stared at Alex, who was frantic. The zombie hand was between the two boys.

Seconds later, the entire top half of the zombie emerged. His eyes looked both at Alex and Johnny the same time; one eye to the left and one to the right. There was green slime everywhere.

The creature was stuck halfway, but Alex still couldn't figure out a way past it to get to the front of the bus. He was shaking and crying. "No, no! Please, I want mommy." He looked helplessly at Johnny.

CHAPTER
13

ver the seats! Hop over the seats!"

Alex didn't move.

The zombie continued wiggling himself free. His arms looked like a sick tree trunk, except in gray.

"Alex! Listen to me. You have to move right now! Or . . ."

But the monster finally made its way onto the bus. As it stood up between Alex and Johnny, it made a sound that was a mixture of a groan and a growl. Johnny noticed how much bigger this zombie was compared to the others they had seen. His head smashed through the ceiling of the bus leaving a narrow skylight. It was obvious this wasn't a normal one—whatever "normal" meant for a zombie.

The zombie set his sights on Alex since he was closer. The monster stepped towards the back of the bus with his left leg, and this time you could hear his bones shake. The windows almost cracked. Then again, he stepped with his right foot on the right side of the bus. Windows exploded. In desperation, Alex yanked on the back emergency exit lever.

The zombie closed in on Alex. Its eyes splashed around in its eye sockets and saliva dripped from his rotten teeth. Just as it was about to engulf him, Alex found the right spot on the handle, yanked the knob up and hard to the left, and the exit door swung open with Alex hanging on like it was the monkey bars at the park.

As the zombie's pointy, cracked fingernails reached for Alex's throat, it fell out of the bus and crashed onto the ground next to Alex. However, since Alex was only seventy pounds he was able to recover more quickly. As he was about to run for cover, the zombie reached out and grabbed a hold of his tiny feet. Alex screamed, kicking, and clawing at the dirt as he fell head first to the ground. His legs started to wiggle. Then seconds later they stopped. He was falling into a trance again, just like this morning. The creature's touch caused it.

CHAPTER
14

HAM!

The large branch broke over the zombie's butt. This caused the creature to let go of Alex and turn around, wondering who swung the branch.

It was Johnny. He looked at the ground and picked up another, unbroken branch. This one was shorter but felt sturdier. Johnny could see that the first branch barely registered as a tickle to the hulking beast. The oversized stick now in his hand probably wouldn't do much more. Nonetheless, he wielded it bravely. He committed to saving his friend as rain began to fall. Hard.

The zombie rose, screaming out a yell so loud that all the birds flew out of the forest up into the sky. The zombie charged at Johnny. Johnny let out his mighty yell and cocked the branch back, ready to let loose.

Before he could swing, the zombie stopped on its own; its face changed from menacing to distracted. Its attention was now elsewhere.

Johnny had no idea what was happening. He heard what it was that stayed the zombie. It was a familiar sound, a great roar, in the distance. A roar one hundred times louder than the zombie on the bus. It was a call.

The zombie stormed right past Johnny. Johnny swung the branch anyway, hitting the zombie in the thigh. The impact did nothing to disrupt the zombie from what seemed to be its greater purpose.

Johnny noticed the caller and was shocked to see it was none other than Ms. Eisenstein. A corrupted, unholy Ms. Eisenstein.

He couldn't believe what he was seeing. Only minutes ago she was as human as he was. Now, it was as if she was some kind of zombie leader, beckoning other zombies.

And they listened indeed. Through the trees, Johnny noticed a host of activity. It was a great migration of zombies all headed in the direction of that same call. They were coming from the city and making their way up into the hills. They were a herd of one mind. Where could they be going?

Then he realized it was to the high grounds of the woods. The fire!

Johnny glanced at Alex from a distance. "Hey, I think I know a faster way," Johnny said, but Alex didn't acknowledge him. Not even a little. "Alex!" He just kept walking. Johnny ran over and stood in front of him, trying to stop his pace.

Alex stopped, but it was as if his eyes were looking *through* Johnny, rather than at him. Johnny realized something, staring at his reflection through Alex's glasses. This was the same kind of trance Alex was in on the bus that morning. But there was something different this time. Alex's skin, it had lost some color. His expression was empty.

"Alex," Johnny said to him again although his voice now had a worry in it. "You there?"

Johnny pinched Alex on the arm like he did on the bus that morning. It didn't work (again).

At the same time, dread was overcoming Johnny. Zombies attacked some people and others, like Alex, could be turned into zombies *by* other zombies. Why does this happen? And how?

But as quickly as the questions entered Johnny's mind, they left, because he realized Alex was, could be, might be . . . a zombie now.

"You snapped out of it this morning," Johnny told him. "You can do it again." Johnny grabbed Alex by the shoulders and shook him. Nothing. Same lifeless glare.

Johnny let go. And when he did, Alex continued his original path into the hills with the rest of the undead clan moving through the bushes. Alex never looked back at Johnny, not once. He disappeared into the darkened forest, taking zombie-like steps, slow and hard. You could hear Alex's tiny bones cracking with each step.

Johnny couldn't afford to keep thinking about it. He had to get to everyone else surrounded by the safe haven of the fire. He had to warn them that evil was coming before it was too late. What else could he do?

He bounded onward, forging his path to the top.

CHAPTER
15

Johnny couldn't tell if it was sweat or rainwater dripping down his face. And he didn't care. He had a bad scrape on his knee from falling a little way's back. He also earned a number of scratches and cuts from charging through the thicket. He didn't care about those either. Johnny followed the smell of burned wood, now overpowering through the wetness.

He was out of breath, pushing himself to get ahead of the zombies on the opposite side. He climbed and leapt, dodged and ducked.

On a regular day, this was beyond his limits, but there may never be another ordinary day after this.

"Hey!" A woman's voice rang through the woods.

Johnny stopped, put his fists up and looked for the person.

"Over here."

It was a face he thought he recognized. As it moved closer, he knew for sure whom it was.

"Mrs. Dupree?" She had long brown hair down to her waist and was wearing a white v-neck t-shirt, tight blue jeans, and mountain boots.

"Johnny!"

Minutes later, Mrs. Dupree grabbed Johnny's arm and rushed him to the clearing at the summit. There must have been hundreds of people scattered around. Many of them were trying to relight the main fire in the dying rainfall. There was yelling and arguing all over. There was also consoling, and planning, and praying. All classes of people were represented: rich and poor, young and old, men and women. All the people at the summit were together, united by a common predator.

"He said, 'They're coming!'" Mrs. Dupree

shouted with two hands cupping her mouth, to anyone within earshot. "They're coming! They're coming!"

These words echoed rapidly through the masses, fueled by utter panic. "They're coming, they're coming." The same parroted words were playing musical chairs with the desperate crowd looking up at Mrs. Dupree and Johnny.

"Stay with me," Mrs. Dupree told Johnny in a quivering voice, grabbing his wrist. "Stay close."

He soon heard that dreaded familiar sound again:

Scratch, scratch, scratch.

Except it had been multiplied hundreds of times and now echoed through the high trees.

Scratch, scratch, scratch. Scratch, scratch, scratch. Scratch, scratch, scratch.

CHAPTER
16
~~~~~~~~~

From Johnny's elevated ground, he could see everything. The zombies began trickling through the trees into the clearing on the opposite end; hundreds upon hundreds of bones clacking, pushing against rotted flesh. The humans retreated from the oncoming horde.

It wasn't long before the entire host took up half of the clearing. Johnny looked down, searching for Alex. He couldn't find him. But he thought he saw others he knew, or, rather, once knew.

Then, all at once, at the sound of an unseen call, they stopped moving forward—like an army waiting to take orders again.

A path began to clear in the middle of the zombies. The frantic humans were on the opposite side. Through the middle came the most fearsome and largest male beast of the whole lot. He marched forward with the clout of a general. He was twelve feet tall, and you could see his bones tighten right through his rotten flesh as he pounded the grass with each step. Green ooze was hanging from every part of his body and his jaw was hanging down by his shoulder with green saliva dripping down.

He came to the front, put his hands on his waist, and looked upon the terrified people. He smirked and spoke, "Humans." His voice was dark, diabolical and otherworldly. "Welcome to your doom."

Shrieks and stirs rang through the crowd.

The big leader paced calmly. "You have but two choices. You can join us, or we can destroy you. It's really up to you. Even if it doesn't feel like it is." He chuckled to himself.

Johnny broke away from Mrs. Dupree's side. "Johnny!" But he was already gone. He slid down the elevated steep, taking a home plate baseball slide through the rocks and mud down to the battle ring.

The leader took another step forward. The frontline of the frantic humans jumped back. He stopped, seemingly amused.

Somewhere behind the leader was Alex. He was just another one of the undead gang staring into space. He peered ahead like everyone else awaiting instruction. This included Coach McGinty, the stranded banker on the roof, and all of the other unfortunate townspeople who were *zombified*.

"So?" The big one continued, scanning around, addressing the humans. "Who's first? Or should I say . . . Who's next? No one? Maybe you need one of your own to set an example." He turned around and signaled to someone unseen. Springing out of the pack and next to Monster Zombie's side was none other than Ms. Eisenstein.

Or at least, some dreadful version of her.

"That's the school bus driver," one of the human voices called out.

"Ms. Eisenstein," said another. "How could she?"

Murmurs of this ran through the crowd.

The bus driver's elected leader kneeled down beside her on one knee. She placed her hand on a piece of his decayed flesh of a shoulder, which was the size of two tree trunks combined. "Who should our next recruit be?" she asked the Monster Zombie. "Or our next meal? Hahahaha," she snickered, almost burping towards the end. "Once we have the majority of the town they can never convert back."

The rest of the zombies livened up at the word "meal." The Zombies started whispering "Meal, meal, meal" through their side of the clearing. Their eyeballs splashed left and right, looking at each of the desperate humans.

With a mere lowering of his hand, the Monster Zombie quieted them as he stood up, looking as tall as the trees. He turned back to his leader, Ms. Eisenstein. "You choose."

At that, Ms. Eisenstein barged forward, taking aim at a girl no older than eighteen on the other side. A man in a delivery truck uniform, her father, stepped in front and braced himself for the attack with his eyes closed. "I say we start with the thin one," Ms. Eisenstein giggled.

CHAPTER
17

All was going according to plan for the zombies until the Monster Zombie caught a whiff of something peculiar. He gave two large sniffs through his putrid nostrils and glanced over the human heads. Immediately, a look of concern appeared on his wretched face. His two eyes went in two different directions and quickly spun. The rest of the zombies cowered back with a sheer look of fright on their faces. Reflected in their dead eyes was the extinguished fire, rising again.

Standing at the base of the flames with blisters on his hand was Johnny. While everyone else was too petrified to think, Johnny caught sight of some dry tinder sticks under a fallen branch. He snatched them and pushed his way toward the pit. That was the moment when he knew his dad's crazy camping trips had come in handy. He knew what to do, focusing on what his father taught him. He set up the sticks perpendicular to each other and began spinning the vertical one furiously. Slowly, and with a punishing amount of effort, wisps of smoke began to rise from the base of the spinning stick.

Moments later, someone from the crowd felt a little heat and looked over. Then others. "He did it! The boy did it!" they shouted as if little Johnny was the chosen one.

"More wood!" another person yelled. The fire rippled some more, growing stronger.

"Make torches!"

Some hasty cooperation produced a few handheld branch flares right away. Those holding one ran forward or passed it to the front. At first, it wasn't much. But it was enough to keep the zombies at bay while more were made.

The creatures—along with Ms. Eisenstein

and Alex—scattered backwards to avoid the one element that could destroy them. Johnny was right about the fires. The flames didn't even have to touch their flesh to burn it. The flames, mixing in the moist air, were powerful enough to burn zombie flesh from a distance. As their flesh was burnt, the air was filled with the foulest of odors.

Soon all the zombies created havoc, yelling and howling for mercy. They immediately fell to their knees, feeling paralyzed. The Monster Zombie was the only one who momentarily held his ground as the brave torchbearers crept forward, reclaiming the clearing. One of the shortest torchbearers was Johnny.

He ran forward, to the front of the pack, receiving pats and high-fives and cheers as he went—like he never did in basketball. He eventually took his place at the vanguard and looked up at the Monster Zombie. His torch created light under the enormous creature's shadow as his slimy gray skin flapped and burned in the wind.

Behind the Monster Zombie, the ringleader crossed her arms, and her right leg was tapping impatiently. The Monster Zombie bent down with flames rushing through his body and got a closer look at this spirited, young boy. His eyes rested on his cheeks. His burnt flesh became darker.

Johnny lifted his torch higher. "Stay right there," he ordered. The Monster Zombie whiplashed his head back away from his flame.

"You think a puny human boy with a little torch in his hand can defeat *me?*" the Monster Zombie thundered. He swiped angrily at Johnny who ducked out of the way. Unfortunately, this caused him to drop his torch. As he crawled on the ground to reach for it, the Monster Zombie stepped in his way, looming over Johnny with a smirk of evil intent.

Out of desperation, Johnny grabbed a large, semi-sharp rock in the nearby soil and jabbed it into the Monster Zombie's foot. The zombie leader seemed amused more than anything. The creature lifted his foot. "I've squashed bigger annoyances than you, puny plebe."

"The name is Johnny."

The Monster Zombie started chuckling. But then the smile turned quickly to a frown. He smelled large amounts of smoke rising directly behind him as he heard a chant cast in the wind. "Johnny, Johnny, Johnny." Turning his head, he roared out another gruesome call that kept the eagles high in the sky. He let out a yelp and fell to the ground trying to put out his flaming rear end.

Johnny looked to see who set the Monster

Zombie's butt on fire. But he couldn't tell because the summit of the forest hill was alight with nearly a hundred torches.

The Monster Zombie knew today would not be his day with his legs on fire and butt in flames. Many of his zombie followers were a step ahead, burning to the ground with nothing but ashes remaining. "Ahhhhhh . . . This is not over," he cried furiously in the wind.

"Oh, no," Johnny said. "You're not going anywhere until you release the transformed humans from their trance."

"You do not make demands on me, boy!" he said in a weakened demonic voice.

A second later, dozens of people holding torches surrounded Johnny, threatening the Monster Zombie further. He stumbled back on his knees and nearly fell over.

As more humans got closer trying to set

the Monster Zombie's head on fire, Johnny saw a shadow in the corner of his eye followed by a familiar sound

Scratch, scratch, scratch.

CHAPTER

18

~~~~~~~~~~~~

Johnny ultimately took his gaze off the large defunct creature and ducked down looking, with one hand cupping his eyes, for the evil, chubby ringleader.

"The only person that can lift the spell is Ms. Eisenstein," he said to himself searching high and low, looking for the witch.

"There she is," Johnny shouted as he ran with the flaming torch in his hand.

Ms. Eisenstein was wobbling slowly through the heard of ashes trying to escape into the forest. "She's too far, and I'm never going to catch her," Johnny thought. As he caught his breath while leaning against a tree branch, he kneeled down to the forest floor and remembered the peanut butter stain on Ms. Eisenstein. "That's right! I'll give her what she can't say no to."

He quickly unzipped his backpack, reached in and grabbed his mom's famous PB&J sandwich. "Got it! Ms. Eisenstein's favorite!" He then remembered what his dad taught him "Right arm back, right foot back, swing from the hip and aim at the chest," as he let the creamy recipe fly through the forest.

BAAM!

He nailed her right on her big butt, causing her to splat down and break her witch heels. The sandwich was unscathed. As Johnny quickly caught up to the ringleader, he noticed her fumbling for something. "You are defeated! You Evil Witch."

As she heard Johnny's brave voice, she rolled over and whacked him with a tree branch nearly hitting his ankles. Luckily, Johnny jumped up and dodged the blow but lost his balance as he fell to the floor. His torch rolled over a few feet.

As she looked in his eyes from the ground, she reached over her shoulder and gripped a tiny silver half-broken metal gadget within her chubby fingers. "This is just the beginning, you little rat." She huffed and raised it to her mouth.

"Hey, is that Coach McGinty's whistle?" Johnny shouted.

"Ha, ha, ha," the evil zombie-leader chuckled on the floor.

"What are you going to do with that?" Johnny questioned.

"You silly boy, tricks are for kids. Ha, ha, ha, ha." She chuckled more, nearly spitting into the cracked, thin, metal whistle.

All of a sudden, Johnny dived into the mud next to Ms. Eisenstein. She looked at him, puzzled, with the whistle between her brown lipstick-shaded lips. He quickly gripped the bottom of the burning torch, got up on one knee, yanked back, and threw the flame, which landed on the peanut butter and jelly sandwich resting to the side of the witch's big butt. The flames spread quickly up her chubby thigh.

POP! BAAM! BOOM!

Ms. Eisenstein's "Ha, ha, ha's" quickly turned to "Ah, ah, ahs" as her skin began decaying off in the fire.

The whistle slid from her fingers and into the dirt. The right side of her body turned into ashes. She reached over with her only functional arm and gripped the whistle just in time as the flames raced to her left arm.

"Fine! Have it your way!" she gave one last chuckle and, *poof*, vanished into ashes. She left a large circle of green slime residue that could have been enough for three or four zombies combined.

Scratch, scratch, scratch.

By now the rain had completely stopped. The fire was stronger than ever and from a distance Alex, Ms. Eisenstein, Coach McGinty came back to life. They all had their heads down between their laps sitting back to back in a circle in the middle of the clearing. Hundreds more scattered behind them. There was a giant circle formed around the converted pack. They all looked dazed as if they couldn't tell what had happened, or how they had gotten there.

Alex was the first to come to his senses and quickly yelled, "Johnny!"

Johnny, from a distance, slowly stood up, wiped the mud off his shirt, and ran to Alex. "Thought I lost you for good, ya big dummy!"

"My bad," was all Alex could muster.

Johnny gave his recovered friend a slap on the shoulder. The two laughed.

Meanwhile, the remaining zombies—the true undead who couldn't be saved—shuffled into the forest, scattered and disappeared into dust as their leader expired in the flames.

CHAPTER
19

Back in Johnny's neighborhood, the wind had died down, and the streets were calm. He opened the door to his house and strutted in with confidence like he never had before.

His mom was in the kitchen preparing dinner. "Where were you, Johnny? You're home later than usual."

Johnny stepped into the kitchen. His clothes were stained and tattered. He was muddied and bruised. He dropped his unzipped backpack on the floor.

When Johnny's mom turned around and saw him, she was startled. "*What* happened to you? It looks like someone enjoyed their sandwich!" She stared at the empty container in the backpack.

Johnny calmly walked past her to the fridge. He opened it, took out a juice box, took the straw out of the plastic and popped it in, taking a long, refreshing sip. After he wiped his mouth, he finally responded to his shocked and confused mother.

"You wouldn't believe me if I told you, Mom."

"Try me," she said, unimpressed.

So Johnny did, from when he got on the bus to when he walked back through the door, a minute go. He didn't spare a single detail.

"You're right," his mom said. "I don't believe you. Go clean up and get ready for dinner." She walked out of the kitchen.

Johnny sat down at the table. Jafree hopped up and rubbed up next to Johnny's knuckles before circling and plopping down on the tabletop. Johnny patted as the cat purred.

"I know you believe me, buddy. That's all that matters."

Then a sound interrupted Johnny's moment of peace. His head lifted up and his eyes widened, looking around.

Scratch, scratch, scratch.

"Was that you, buddy?" Johnny asked the cat nervously stroking him between the ears.

Jafree only glanced up at him from the table before laying his head back down, "Purr, grrr." Jafree stood up, stretched, and jumped into Johnny's lap and curled into a ball.

THE END

ABOUT
THE AUTHOR

~~~~~~~~~~

A.M. Shah is an author of several picture and chapter books. When he's not briefing dense cases that make his eyeballs splash out of his sockets during law school, he's writing spooky fiction for kids. He lives with his wife, Dr. Melissa Arias Shah, a prominent psychotherapist, and their two children, Ashton and Ashley, in Miami, Florida.

CPSIA information can be obtained at www.ICGtesting.com
Printed in the USA
LVOW08s2354061016

507769LV00001B/143/P

9 781943 684182